0 026 460 12X 4E

This item must be returned or renewed on or before the latest date shown

13/2/10

2 9 SEP 2010

5/7/11

4/4/12   2 5 SEP 2012

8/2/14   2 3 SEP 2017

17/8

2¢/8/22.

Renew online at http://www.catalogue.sefton.gov.uk/.

Or by telephone at any Sefton library:

Bootle: 0151 934 5781          Meadows: 0151 288 6727

Crosby: 0151 257 6400        Netherton: 0151 525 0607

Formby: 01704 874177        Southport: 0151 934 2118

A fine will be charged on any overdue item plus the cost of reminders sent

MJW          £4.99

You do not need to read this page –
just get on with the book!

Published in 2006 in Great Britain by
Barrington Stoke Ltd
18 Walker St, Edinburgh, EH3 7LP

www.barringtonstoke.co.uk

Reprinted 2007 (twice), 2009

ISBN: 978-1-84299-356-9

Printed in Great Britain by Bell & Bain Ltd

## MEET THE AUTHOR – TONY BRADMAN

*What is your favourite animal?*
**Whales**
*What is your favourite boy's name?*
**Thomas (my son's name)**
*What is your favourite girl's name?*
**Sally, Emma and Helen (my wife and daughters)**
*What is your favourite food?*
**Grilled fish**
*What is your favourite music?*
**The Beatles**
*What is your favourite hobby?*
**Going to the cinema**

## MEET THE ILLUSTRATOR – KAREN DONNELLY

*What is your favourite animal?*
**Woodlice!**
*What is your favourite boy's name?*
**Laurie**
*What is your favourite girl's name?*
**Jean**
*What is your favourite food?*
**Sausages and runny eggs**
*What is your favourite music?*
**Beck**
*What is your favourite hobby?*
**Drawing and printmaking**

# Contents

# Chapter 1
# Robbie's Dream

As Robbie Jones rode his bike round the park one Sunday morning, he saw a boys' football team coming out onto the sports' pitch. It was love at first sight. Robbie had always wanted to play football for a real team, and he had seen lots of them play – but he knew at once that this was the one for him.

These kids were the same age as him, but they trotted towards the pitch in a line just like a Premiership side. Their green and black strip was pretty cool. Each player's shirt had his number on it and his name. They had a proper coach, too – a big man in a track suit with a very loud voice and a red face. He was getting them to do lots of warm-up exercises before play started – just as if they were a Premiership side.

There were some dads watching from the touchline. There were a few mums too and some little brothers and sisters. There was also an older man with a clipboard. Robbie left his bike by a tree, and went over to ask him what the team's name was.

"Top Grove FC," the man replied. "They're playing Forest Hill Athletics F.C. It's just a friendly, but I hope it'll be a good game …"

It wasn't. It was scrappy and dull, but Robbie didn't care. He had lots more questions to ask. The man with the clipboard was very helpful and by the end of the match – a messy goal gave Top Grove a 1-0 win – Robbie knew plenty about the team he wanted to join.

One thing he knew was that Top Grove F.C. were playing in a new league. The man with the clipboard – Robbie called him Mr Clipboard – was the league's secretary. The big coach with the red face was a wealthy businessman called Mr Jenkins. His son, Duncan, was Top Grove's captain.

As soon as the game was over Robbie took a deep breath, grabbed his bike and headed off to talk to the Top Grove players.

"You were brill, Dunc!" Robbie heard someone say. *That's odd*, thought Robbie. Duncan hadn't really had *that* good a game.

"Er … hi," said Robbie. He felt rather shy. The group fell silent, and turned to stare at him. "I wanted to find out … how do I join your team …?"

"What school do you go to?" said Duncan. He took a step forward.

"Sunny Bank," muttered Robbie.

"Really?" said Duncan. He looked over at Robbie's battered old bike, then down at Robbie's cheap, scruffy trainers. "I think we've got all the players we need at the moment, haven't we, guys?"

Robbie heard someone snigger, and felt his cheeks burn.

He trudged away, past Mr Jenkins and Mr Clipboard, who were arguing. The team that was meant to play against Top Grove in the friendly next Sunday had pulled out.

Mr Jenkins wanted another team to replace them, and Mr Clipboard couldn't find one.

# Chapter 2
# Brainwave?

Robbie rode his bike out of the park and went home. He shut himself in his bedroom. *It wasn't fair*, he thought. OK, so Duncan Jenkins was posh, and rich. But he could still have given Robbie a chance ... He thought about all this for a long time upstairs in his bedroom. He went on thinking about how unfair it all was right through Sunday lunch. Even after that, when he was sitting in the front room

between his mum and dad. They didn't notice his mood. They were busy arguing.

"I'm fed up with you always deciding what we watch on TV," Mum was saying. "If it isn't blasted men kicking a ball, it's blasted men running around shooting at each other. What *is* this rubbish we're watching now, anyway?"

"It's called *The Dirty Dozen*," Dad replied with a long sigh. "It's a classic. It's all about an American officer who leads a team of soldiers on a special mission behind enemy lines. Got it?"

Mum still wasn't happy. She went on nagging at his dad and saying how *she* wanted to choose what they watched. But Robbie wasn't listening any more. The film had given him an idea. *The Dirty Dozen*, a team on a special mission ... A dozen was 12. There were a dozen players in a football team, 11 plus a substitute. If he could get a team together and play in it – he could show Top Grove what he could do! Robbie sat up, suddenly very excited.

"See?" said Dad to Mum and pointed at Robbie. "He thinks this film's great."

Robbie remembered the row between Mr Jenkins and Mr Clipboard – Top Grove didn't have anyone to play against next Sunday. If *he* could get a team together ... Top Grove could play against them.

He looked back at the TV. In the film, the hero was talking to his second-in-command who was the kind of trusty friend heroes always have.

Suddenly Robbie thought of *his* best friend, Gary. He would help.

"Just popping out to see Gary," he said, and jumped up.

"Traitor," muttered Dad to Robbie as Mum grabbed the remote and switched channels.

Robbie got on his bike and rode to Gary's house. Gary's big brother, Jack, answered the door. "All right, Robbie?" he growled as he opened the door. Jack had hit puberty in a big way. His voice had already broken. Now he talked in such a low, deep voice he sounded as if he could do the talking for horror movie trailers.

"Gary's upstairs," Jack said as Robbie locked up his bike.

Robbie waited on the landing outside his friend's room for a few seconds. He suddenly felt less sure. What was he going to tell Gary? Robbie knew he wasn't the only one who wanted to play proper football in a real team. Gary and his other mate, Nadim, did too. They hated the fact that their school, Sunny Bank, didn't have a team. Maybe *they* would like a chance to show Top Grove what they could do ... They were good players as well.

Robbie knew he was a good footballer – but was he making things difficult for himself? Would his friends play better than he did? He'd played football in the school playground with his mates for years, so he knew some of them could be pretty impressive. They might even look better than him on the day ...

*No*, he thought, *it will be best to keep my plan secret.* He wouldn't tell Gary or anyone that he wanted to put together a team so that he could show off his own skills to Top Grove. He would tell Gary this was a one-off, the chance to play a proper game, just once and no more than that. Then, if the plan worked, and Top Grove did pick him, Robbie would just act surprised.

For the second time that day Robbie took a deep breath. Then he pushed open Gary's door. Gary turned to smile at him. Robbie felt a bit, just a bit, mean about what he was doing. But he stuck to his plan, anyway, and told Gary about getting a team together.

"I'm not sure, Robbie," said Gary. "Even if we *could* put a team together ... No-one we know has ever played a proper game, have they? I don't even have any proper boots. We'd probably get slaughtered, beaten good and proper."

"We might not," Robbie said. "I bet we'd be good." But in secret he was thinking that, apart from him, the players shouldn't be *too* good. No, he, Robbie, would have the

chance to shine. Out loud Robbie said, "Maybe you could borrow some boots?"

"OK, you're on," said Gary at last. "But who's going to phone this Mr Jenkins to arrange the game? He'll only want to talk to an adult."

"I suppose we could always ask your dad," Gary went on. "He likes football, doesn't he?"

"I don't want to ask him," said Robbie quickly. "I, er ... think it's best if we do this on our own without our parents."

Gary looked puzzled. Then he gave a shrug.

"We do know someone who *sounds* like a grown-up," Robbie added. "Jack could pretend to be our coach."

It didn't take much to get Jack to ring for them. All they had to do was promise to get the phone number of a boy in their class for him. A boy with an older sister that Jack fancied.

There were a few Mr Jenkins in the phone book when Robbie and Gary looked up to find the number. They made a few calls to the wrong Mr Jenkins and then, at last, they found the right one. Jack talked to him for a few moments and fixed it all up.

"There you go, lads," Jack said to them. "Kick off ten-thirty next Sunday morning."

"*Yes!*" said Robbie, and raised a fist. He was on his way ...

# Chapter 3
# Time to Train

Robbie and Gary rang their mates the next morning. Everyone was up for the game, and Robbie soon had a list of 12 names, with his own and Gary's at the top. Robbie decided to set up a training session, too. If the team did get slaughtered, if Top Grove beat them hollow, no-one would look at his skills. He wouldn't get the chance to show them off. He needed his side to have some idea of how to play as a team.

The training session was set for Tuesday. Gary ticked everyone off the list as they arrived – Wayne, Lefty, Luke, Big Dan, Billy, Jez, Nadim, Willsy, Darren and Martin. All the boys were excited, and stood around chattering. Then, of course, came the arguments about who should play in what position.

This was something Robbie hadn't thought about. He wanted to play as a striker, his dream spot. But now he saw that if he didn't take control of things, he could end up playing anywhere.

"*Quiet!*" he yelled. Everybody fell silent and stared at him. "This was my idea, so I am in charge, and *I'll* decide who plays where."

There was some grumbling, but soon everyone was quiet again. "Right, Luke," Robbie went on, "you're in goal ..."

It didn't take Robbie long to put the side together. He knew how all his friends played – who was good at what. He knew who could shoot, who could head the ball, who could tackle. And, of course, he gave himself the position he wanted.

He'd promised the lads some training, so now he set up a six-a-side game of attackers against defenders. They played for a bit but soon the game turned into a kick-about – which was fine by Robbie. But it wasn't OK with Gary.

"You'll have to be a bit firmer with us in tomorrow's session, Robbie," Gary said when the game was over and everyone was drifting off home. "I mean, that game was fun, but we didn't make much progress as a team, did we? We'll have to do better than that tomorrow."

"Tomorrow?" said Robbie. This wasn't part of his plan.

"Maybe we could go to the library on the way home and get out some of those coaching videos to give us ideas," said Gary. "And some books, too."

"I wasn't planning on us doing any more training," said Robbie.

"You what?" said Gary. Then he laughed. "You're joking, right?"

"Huh, can't fool you, can I, Gary?" said Robbie with a stiff smile.

So Robbie arranged some more training sessions. They trained on Wednesday, on Thursday, and on Friday. Thanks to Gary and his coaching videos and football books, they knew what they had to practise too. They had a last session on Saturday morning and agreed to meet in the park at ten o'clock the next day. Then they all went home.

Gary and Robbie rode their bikes together as far as Robbie's house.

"You know, Robbie, I've been thinking," said Gary. "It's funny how things turn out, isn't it? I mean, if you and I hadn't been made to sit together when we started school, we might never have become friends."

"No, I suppose not," said Robbie. He couldn't see why Gary was talking about them starting school.

"And if we weren't friends, then you probably wouldn't have asked me to play in this game," Gary went on, "and it could be the biggest, most exciting day of my life. So

I just want to say ... thanks, Robbie. Thanks for being such a good mate."

"Don't go on about it," said Robbie. "Please *don't* go on about it ..."

Gary gave him a puzzled look, then rode off home.

# Chapter 4
# Traitor

The next morning Robbie got up, had breakfast, put his kit in a Tesco's bag, and set off through drizzly rain to the park. The bag with his kit hung from his handlebars and banged against his knees.

The other lads soon arrived, and so did Mr Clipboard.

"I take it you're Top Grove's mystery opponents," he said. He looked at everyone in the team and saw Robbie. "Hold on, don't I know you?" he said. Then he gave a shrug. "Oh, never mind. If you'll just point me towards your coach ..."

"Er ... He can't make it today, I'm afraid," said Robbie. *Mostly because he doesn't exist*, he thought. "We're looking after ourselves," he added.

"I see," said Mr Clipboard. "This is all very odd. It's not what happens normally. First your coach contacts Top Grove direct, instead of me as he should have done, and now I find out he's not even here! Tell me, what's the *name* of your team?"

"Their coach didn't give me a name," boomed a voice behind them. Mr Jenkins had also arrived. "To be frank, I don't care *what* they are called so long as they're changed and ready by ten-thirty. Can we get on with it?"

"I suppose so," said Mr Clipboard in a cross voice. "Although there's no need to be so rude," he muttered.

"This way, boys ..." Mr Clipboard shouted to Robbie and his mates and pointed to the park sports sheds. Inside was a big room with benches round the walls, and coat-hooks above. There was a lot of nervous laughter as they got changed, and a few jokes about Mr Jenkins. Then it was time for Robbie to lead them out.

The rain had stopped, but as Robbie ran on to the pitch he saw the ground was quite muddy. The pitch seemed bigger too. It was odd to see the same things as last week but now in such a different way. There were the dads and mums and little brothers and sisters standing on the touchline ...

And there were the Top Grove players in their black and green shirts. They were sniggering at Robbie and the rest of his team, and they didn't care who saw. Robbie looked at his mates' scruffy kit. Everyone had different strips on. They had odd socks and cheap or old boots they'd borrowed from friends. Robbie felt his cheeks burning again. Next to the Top Grove side, Robbie's team looked a mess.

"Right, can I have the two captains, please?" someone called out.

It was Mr Clipboard. He had changed, too, into a proper referee's strip. Robbie trotted over to him in the centre circle, and so did Duncan Jenkins.

Duncan stared at Robbie, then smirked. "Well, well," he said. "I wasn't expecting *you* back so soon. Are you that keen to show me what you can do? Maybe I *should* give you a trial after all. On second thoughts, I'll see you play first."

"What's he talking about, Robbie?" said Gary.

Robbie turned round. Gary was standing nearby, and he was scowling at Robbie. Robbie opened his mouth to say something, but just then Mr Clipboard started talking about the coin toss. Robbie had to pay attention. He lost the toss and Duncan chose to kick off. Mr Clipboard put the ball down on the centre spot, and the teams got into position for the start of the game.

"Listen, Gary ..." said Robbie as he moved back into midfield.

"Spare me the excuses," Gary snapped. "I *knew* there was something funny about this. You didn't want to do any more training ... you didn't want our parents to know … you set this game up so you could get into the Top Grove team! Hah! Some friend *you* turned out to be."

Mr Clipboard blew his whistle as Gary finished speaking, and the game began. *Just as well we're playing now*, thought Robbie. He didn't have a clue what to say. Gary had Robbie sussed – he'd worked it all out. Robbie felt sick. He saw Willsy and Nadim and Jez scowling too. They must have heard Gary.

Then someone bumped into him, and sent him flying.

"Whoops, sorry!" said Duncan. "I hope I didn't wake you up …"

Robbie never forgot that first half. It was the first time he'd played proper football on a proper pitch. It was a total nightmare. Top Grove were unlucky not to score straight away. Duncan took a pass from the edge of the box. If he'd hit the ball better, Robbie's goalkeeper, Luke, would have had no chance. But Duncan's shot skidded wide.

But there was no let-up and soon Top Grove were all over Robbie and the lads like a rash. Shots rained in on Luke's goal, and Robbie was amazed none of them went in. He and his team mates simply couldn't get any possession, and they spent their whole time chasing the Top Grove players. *This is crazy*, thought Robbie at last, and stopped running.

He looked at his team. They were supposed to be playing 4-4-2. Nadim, Wayne, Big Dan, Billy and Lefty were the back four. Willsy, Luke, Gary and Robbie were the midfield, and Martin and Jez were upfront. Darren was the sub. But Robbie's team had lost its shape – they were all out of position, and getting in each other's way. *What a mess*, thought Robbie.

So far *he'd* done nothing but miss tackles and fall over. He hadn't put in any good passes yet, or hit a decent shot. He'd hardly been in Top Grove's half. Duncan just laughed when he was near him. There was another problem, too. The whole team seemed to know now what Gary had said. Even Darren, the sub, waiting on the touchline knew. They were all scowling.

Then, of course, it happened. As Robbie watched, a Top Grove attack built up on the right-hand side. Robbie started running again as a Top Grove player put in a cross. Someone had got a head to it, then the ball came down in the area, and a second later ... it was over the line into goal. Top Grove had scored, and Duncan raised his arms to the sky and cheered.

"Great goal, Duncan!" bellowed Mr Jenkins. "*Smashing* goal!"

That's odd, thought Robbie. He was certain Duncan hadn't got the final touch. But everyone in the Top Grove team seemed happy to let him take the credit – and suddenly Robbie understood why. *They had to.* I bet Mr Jenkins started the team for Duncan, he thought. And the price for getting your name on the black and green shirts ... was to make Duncan feel like he was the best player.

As Jez lost the ball from the re-start, Robbie was still thinking and worked something out. Mr Jenkins had got Top Grove F.C. together because Duncan thought he was a good player and wanted to show off. Robbie saw how Duncan kept calling for the ball, and doing tricks with it, and showing off for the people watching on the touchline. *But then*, thought Robbie, *he was just as bad.* Robbie had got a team together, too, so that *he* could show off his skills. He couldn't slag off Duncan because he was doing just the same thing. But all he'd done was upset his best friend, and his other mates. Robbie remembered that word Dad had used – *traitor* ... And in the end, it had all been for nothing. Robbie saw Duncan bustling one of his own players off the ball. He saw that there would never be any truly good players at Top Grove FC, or anyone who couldn't take orders from Duncan or Mr Jenkins.

*This match was a total waste of time and effort*, Robbie thought. Worse than that, he'd made a real fool of himself ...

A few moments later Mr Clipboard blew his whistle for half-time. Robbie's mates slowly got together in the centre circle, and stood in a tight huddle with their backs to

Robbie. Top Grove headed for the other end of the pitch.

"Well, *you* were pretty useless," said Duncan as he walked past Robbie with his players. "But then I always thought you would be. I mean, what can you expect from someone who goes to a school like Sunny Bank?"

Robbie heard more sniggering as they walked away ... and suddenly he felt very angry. Who the hell did Duncan Jenkins think he was, talking to him like that? What made *him* so special? A father with enough money to *buy* him a team?

# Chapter 5
# Forgiven

*It was time to take Duncan Jenkins down a peg or two*, Robbie thought. He turned and marched off towards his team mates.

"You all right, son?" said Mr Clipboard as Robbie went by him.

"I'm *fine*," said Robbie grimly.

"Second half kicks off in five minutes ..." said Mr Clipboard.

Robbie didn't reply. He kept on walking, and finally stopped near his mates. The huddle of players turned to Robbie and Gary was standing right in the middle. Ten pairs of stern, angry eyes glared up at Robbie. None of his friends spoke.

"I know what you're thinking," said Robbie, "and you've got every reason to hate me. I *did* set this whole thing up to get into Top Grove, and now I'm really sorry. You're my mates. I know now I'd rather play with you than those creeps, OK? Even if it's only for one last half. So let's get out there and show them what the lads from Sunny Bank can *really* do."

Robbie didn't give anyone a chance to argue. He turned round and walked quickly towards the goal they'd be defending, and stood there kicking at the penalty spot. He saw Mr Clipboard looking at him and he saw his mates talking to each other, and looking over at him, too. At last, Mr Clipboard called for the second half to begin.

For a moment Robbie thought his mates weren't going to play ... They stayed huddled together. But, in the end, the huddle broke up, and they drifted to their positions. Darren came on instead of Billy, as the team had decided. Top Grove were ready, too. Mr Clipboard blew his whistle, and Jez tapped the ball to Martin. A Top Grove player came in for a tackle, and the ball squirted out to Duncan, who was ready for it, with a smirk on his face.

*This half it's going to be different*, thought Robbie. He raced up to the ball to put in a tackle of his own. He swept the ball from Duncan's toes and ran on with it.

Duncan went down and appealed to the referee. "Foul, ref!" he shouted.

"No foul!" yelled Mr Clipboard, and waved his arms. "Play on!"

Robbie was on the edge of the Top Grove box now. Their midfielders were chasing him, and their defenders were looking nervous. He jigged past one, then laid the ball off to Martin. Martin thumped in a shot. The Top Grove goalie fell on the ball.

"Keep your shape when they come forward, lads!" Robbie turned and yelled to his side, as the goalie rolled the ball to the nearest defender. Robbie saw that Duncan wasn't grinning any more. That was good. "*Keep ... your ... shape!*" Robbie shouted again.

Robbie's team did keep their shape. Robbie kept reminding them. His anger gave him lots more energy and he tore all over the pitch. He put in lots of tackles and chased all the Top Grove players hard. He shouted to his mates to keep it going. It worked. They started talking to each other, calling for passes or cover. And they made good runs off the ball when the team was in possession.

Top Grove didn't know what had hit them. Robbie began to see just how useful the training sessions and Gary's videos and football books had been. *We've got to score, soon*, Robbie thought ... And then it happened.

Big Dan got the ball and hit it to Nadim. Nadim took it down the left-hand side into the corner, then turned in sharply. He got past a defender easily, and drove the ball hard and low into the box. Robbie was there. He'd run in from midfield, and met the cross sweetly on the half volley. He knocked the ball into goal. One all.

Robbie didn't stop to celebrate. He turned round to go back for Top Grove's re-start – but he was flattened by all his team mates. They'd rushed up to mob him. "Goal! Goal!" they shouted. They were all there – except Gary. Robbie's team's second goal came pretty quickly. Mr Jenkins was bellowing at *his* team so much that they started to get desperate and forgot to play proper football. Duncan knocked Jez down on the edge of the box. Mr Clipboard gave the team a free kick. Willsy blasted a shot into the wall, the ball came back to Robbie. Robbie curled the ball round the goal into the net. 2-1.

But that wasn't the best moment. The best moment came right at the end.

Wayne knocked a long ball up to Willsy, and Willsy flicked it to Robbie. Robbie looked round, and saw Duncan running in to close him down. Robbie waited, nutmegged him, and headed for goal. Then Gary raced in from midfield beside him. Robbie dummied one defender, then a second, and only had the keeper to beat. If he could score and get a hat trick ... Now that really *would* be something ...

Robbie knew he could do it, too. But instead he got the keeper, and laid the ball off for his best friend to score. 3-1 – Gary had scored.

This time Gary was the first in the mob that rushed to flatten Robbie.

"I take it this means I'm forgiven," Robbie said, happy at last.

"Forgiven for what?" said Gary, and grinned at him.

Robbie grinned back.

Just then Mr Clipboard blew three blasts on his whistle for full-time. A cheer went up from Robbie's mates. He and Gary joined in, then high-fived each other with a loud ... "*Yes!*"

Duncan and his team slunk away. Mr Jenkins' face was even redder than normal.

"Could I have a word, lads?" shouted Mr Clipboard as he jogged towards Robbie's team. "I thought you were terrific in that second half. You're just the kind of team we want in the league. I was thinking – would you like to join?"

"Well, I, er ..." Robbie muttered.

"Look I've already worked out that you don't have a coach, but that doesn't matter," said Mr Clipboard. "I'll find you one, and a sponsor as well – the local paper's been looking for a team to buy proper strips for. If you can play like that against Top Grove a couple of times a season, it'll be worth it! And it'll keep old Jenkins quiet, too. Is it a deal?"

"Yes!" said Robbie. Gary was nodding, too.

"Good," said Mr Clipboard. "Here's my card – get your parents to ring me so we can get things started. Oh, and I *will* need a name for your team if I'm to plan your league fixtures. What's it to be?"

Robbie thought for a second. Sunny Bank United? Council Estate FC? No … he looked at his team mates. Their scruffy kits were covered in mud, and they were

laughing and jumping about as if they were mad.

"You can call us ... the Dirty Dozen FC," he said with a smile.

It just seemed right somehow.

Barrington Stoke would like to thank all its readers for commenting on the manuscript before publication and in particular:

Sophie-Louise Armstrong
Aaron Austin
Antony Bliss
Shane Brooks
Stacey Burgess
Julie Carss
Matthew Carvell
James Cox
Sophie Cresswell
Yvonne Farrell
Curtis Fogelberg
Ellie Gray
Yvonne Grundy
William Harrison
Zak Jooyandeh
Berke Kerimologu

Jamie Lees
Greg Madero
Michael McKay
Jopseph O'Callaghan
Danny Purtell
Paige Riley
Ciaran Rogers
Simone
Harlie Swann
Dominic Taylor
Mrs Lynne Varley
Cameron Wardle
Edmund Whitmore
Joshua Wignall
Jacob Wise

## Become a Consultant!

Would you like to give us feedback on our titles before they are published? Contact us at the email address below – we'd love to hear from you!

info@barringtonstoke.co.uk
www.barringtonstoke.co.uk

# Great reads – no problem!

Barrington Stoke books are:

**Great stories** – funny, scary or exciting – and all by the best writers around!

**No hassle** – fast reads with no boring bits, and a brilliant story that you can't put down.

**Short** – the perfect size for a fast, fun read.

We use our own font and paper to make it easier for dyslexic people to read our books too. And we ask readers like you to check every book before it's published.

That way, we know for sure that every Barrington Stoke book is a great read for everyone.

Check out www.barringtonstoke.co.uk for more info about Barrington Stoke and our books!

# If you liked this book, why don't you read ...

# Mixed Up Madness
## by
## Tony Bradman and Alison Prince

## Two great books in one!

In *The Two Jacks* by Tony Bradman, a new teacher mixes up Jack Baker the Perfect Pupil and Jack Barker the Bad Boy, and both Jacks find out what it's like to be different.

In *Screw Loose* by Alison Prince, Roddy sets out to take his useless school apart, but ends up in the headmaster's chair trying to put the school back together!

**You can order *Mixed Up Madness* directly from our website at www.barringtonstoke.co.uk**